This igloo book belongs to:

....

igloobooks

Published in 2019
by Igloo Books Ltd, Cottage Farm, Sywell, NN6 0BJ
www.igloobooks.com

Copyright © 2017 Igloo Books Ltd

Written by Lucy Barnard
Illustrated by Hannah Wood

Cover designed by Nicholas Gage
Interiors designed by Kerri-Ann Hulme
Edited by Caroline Richards

GUA006 1218
4 6 8 10 9 7 5
ISBN 978-1-78670-642-3

Printed and manufactured in China

It Wasn't Me!

igloobooks

But Ella and Oscar's mum and dad weren't silly and they knew...

... that Patch the dog was **not** to blame, it really wasn't true.

When Mum invited her **snooty** friends around for tea.

SPLAT!

went Oscar's ball, right into the pink jelly.

Dad was busy painting when Ella **whizzed** past him, **WHOOSH!**

She made the ladder **wobble** and Dad fell into the bush.

Ella said,

It wasn't me! Patch really wanted us to race.

But she quickly disappeared when she saw Dad's grumpy face.

When Mum baked a chocolate cake,
Oscar thought it looked so **yummy.**

He only meant to sneak one
piece, but it tasted far too
scrummy!

Ella just loved to...

she'd race around...

... **run** and **twirl**,

... and **leap!**

But when she slipped on the wet grass...

... she landed in a **heap.**

One day, Oscar and Ella were having great **fun** at the beach. But as they dug the castle moat, they heard a sudden...

...**screech!**

The sand was in Mum's hair and on Dad's ice-cream cone.

Oscar said,

It wasn't us! Patch was burying his bone!

Back at home, Mum sighed,
"I think there's only one thing we can do."
"You're right," said Dad, looking grim,
"come on over here you two."

"Mum and I have had a chat, we both agree and so,
if all these things are Patch's fault then...

... he'll just have to go!"

They told the **truth** and asked their mum and dad if Patch could stay.

"**On one condition,**" said Dad, "**no more telling lies, okay?**"

The next day Patch was playing...

... but he **slid** on the rug and CRASH!

He **slammed** into the table
and Mum's vase fell with a...

... SMASH!

Oscar gasped and said,

Patch really did do that, but Mum must never know.

Ella said,

You're right, or she might say that Patch will have to go.

So Oscar and Ella took the blame, as Mum cleared the mess away.

Then they had to help around the house doing **boring** jobs all day!

Ella looked over at Oscar as they dusted the bookcase.

Had they really seen a cheeky
grin on little Patch's face?